little Miss Scary

originated by Roger Hargreaves

Written and illustrated by Adam Hargreaves

PSS!
PRICE STERN SLOAN
An Imprint of Penguin Group (USA) Inc.

Little Miss Scary lived near the top of a mountain in a house called Spooky Cottage.

When it was dark she would creep into the valley below, making sure that nobody saw her . . .

And there she would wait very quietly until somebody came along . . .

And when that somebody did, she would tiptoe up behind them, open her mouth wide, and shout . . .

"BOO!"

And do you know why Little Miss Scary did this?

For fun.

You see, she loved to scare people more than anything else in the world.

And she was very good at it.

She scared them stiff.

"BOO!"

She scared them out of their wits.

"BOO!"

She even scared them right out of their socks.

"BOO!"

About a week ago, Mr. Noisy went to see his friend Mr. Nervous.

Mr. Noisy was worried because he hadn't heard from his friend for a while.

When he got to Mr. Nervous's house, he knocked on the door.

Spookily, the door swung open by itself.

"Hello," called Mr. Noisy as softly as he could, which for you or me would have been a shout.

Then he heard a chattering noise coming from the bedroom.

Mr. Noisy found Mr. Nervous hiding under his bed, his teeth chattering in fear.

"Whatever's the . . ." began Mr. Noisy, and then he remembered himself. "Whatever's the matter, Mr. Nervous?"

"It's . . . it's . . . L-L-Little Miss S-S-Scary," chattered Mr. Nervous, trembling in fear. "Sh-sh-she keeps jumping out and shouting 'b-b-b-boo' at me."

Mr. Noisy made Mr. Nervous a cup of tea, calmed him down, and told him what they were going to do.

Just as it was getting dark, they hid behind a bush beside the street that led up to Mr. Nervous's house.

They waited until they saw Little Miss Scary's shadowy figure creeping past them.

Then Mr. Noisy and Mr. Nervous crept out from their hiding place, tiptoed up behind Little Miss Scary, and, at the tops of their voices, shouted . . .

"BOO!"

Now, the top of Mr. Noisy's voice is a very loud place indeed.

So loud that Little Miss Scary leaped five feet in the air and when she came down she ran for her life.

She didn't stop running until she was hidden under her bed.

In her bedroom.

In Spooky Cottage.

At the top of the mountain.

"I don't think you'll be seeing much of her for a long while, Mr. Nervous," chuckled Mr. Noisy. "Mr. Nervous? Mr. Nervous . . . ?"

But there was no sign of Mr. Nervous either.

Mr. Noisy chuckled again and walked back to
Mr. Nervous's house. To have a look under
Mr. Nervous's bed!